CRACKS, DOORS, WINDOWS
and a
STORY-TELLING TREE

L. PETER JONES

BALBOA
PRESS
A DIVISION OF HAY HOUSE

Copyright © 2019 L. Peter Jones.

All rights reserved. No part of this book may be used or reproduced by any means, graphic, electronic, or mechanical, including photocopying, recording, taping or by any information storage retrieval system without the written permission of the author except in the case of brief quotations embodied in critical articles and reviews.

Balboa Press books may be ordered through booksellers or by contacting:

Balboa Press
A Division of Hay House
1663 Liberty Drive
Bloomington, IN 47403
www.balboapress.co.uk
1 (877) 407-4847

Because of the dynamic nature of the Internet, any web addresses or links contained in this book may have changed since publication and may no longer be valid. The views expressed in this work are solely those of the author and do not necessarily reflect the views of the publisher, and the publisher hereby disclaims any responsibility for them.

The author of this book does not dispense medical advice or prescribe the use of any technique as a form of treatment for physical, emotional, or medical problems without the advice of a physician, either directly or indirectly. The intent of the author is only to offer information of a general nature to help you in your quest for emotional and spiritual well-being. In the event you use any of the information in this book for yourself, which is your constitutional right, the author and the publisher assume no responsibility for your actions.

Any people depicted in stock imagery provided by Getty Images are models, and such images are being used for illustrative purposes only.
Certain stock imagery © Getty Images.

Print information available on the last page.

ISBN: 978-1-9822-8088-8 (sc)
ISBN: 978-1-9822-8089-5 (e)

Balboa Press rev. date: 07/26/2019

CONTENTS

THE CRACK IN THE WALL

Dedication 1
Acknowledgement 3
One 5
Two 7
Three 11
Four 15
Five 17
Six 21
Seven 24

IGOR'S MONSTER

Dedication 29
One 31
Two 33
Three 35
Four 37
Five 39
Six 40

THE STORY-TELLING TREE

Dedication 43
Acknowledgements..45
One.. 47
Two.. 59
Three.. 71
Four.. 78
Five... 83

THE CRACK IN THE WALL

DEDICATION

This short story is dedicated to three important people:

Claudette, whose warm, welcoming café, *Poppy's*, serves the most delicious meals and the most mouth-watering deserts, and who inspired me to write again; Pema Chrodron, whose books taught me that life and truth and beauty will always survive; and to Patrick Brook, whose advice and wise words supported me through very difficult times.

ACKNOWLEDGEMENT

I acknowledge my inspiration from
work by Pema Chodron.

ONE

Joanna's parents built the house that she lived in. In fact, they had started the house long, long before Joanna was even born, from ancient plans that their own parents had given them.

Completing the house while Joanna was still only a child, they could not stop themselves from adding bits here or there, whenever the mood or inclination took them, until the house stood as it did now, indomitable, strong and impenetrable, a safe haven for Joanna, a sanctuary, something akin to a kind, old womb.

To Joanna, the 'House', as it slowly became known, was a captivating servant. It seemed to serve her every comfort and need, and its endless practicality, its order and predictability, was to her a form of intricate, seductive beauty. The House was also a place of utter reliability and an unchanging, uncomplaining backcloth, which kept her unquestioning-safe.

Obviously, Joanna became intimate with the House's every nook and cranny; she loved every wall and crevice and she knew every spot and shelf. Joanna also knew its every subtlety: where it was lightest, and where there were shadows; where it seemed she could run free and where corridors came to an end. There was no place in the house to feel forgotten, no place to hide, no place for doubt.

This was the House and it looked after her.

TWO

Late one morning, Joanna felt the edges of boredom creeping round her like a cloak, so she decided, on a whim, that what she needed to cure her tight-lipped unease was to spend some time in the library.

The library was not that far from where Joanna happened to be and where she spent most of her time – the cosy core of the House. But the library was as far as you could go in a house built in several concentric circles because it was situated on the outer rim, the place closest to the outside and furthest from the centre.

Once decided, Joanna brightened and she energetically tucked away a trailing strand of hair and straightened her long buttoned dress. Order had been restored, and she was ready for the trek. She had not visited the library in some while and she set off with a certain spring in her step and a few finished books beneath her arm.

Arriving in the library, she noticed immediately that something was wrong. One of the books, from the shelf that dealt with rules and regulations, the proper ordinance of the House itself, was sagging, hanging out of place, a place it had held from the beginning. It was like seeing a respected priest drunk and swearing in the middle of a packed street and everyone staring not knowing quite what to do. Years of changeless order and neat regularity had come, brutally, to an unexpected end. Joanna experienced in a heart beat a moment of confusion and anger, then shock and inaction. So she froze. But then blinking away this miasma of feeling, Joanna went to investigate. Was it something she had done? Something she had not done?

Joanna reached for a small three-legged stool, which brought her to within reach of the offending tome.

Joanna touched the book and her sensitive fingers pulled away violently. The book was soaking wet and heavy droplets poured from it – it was like touching putrid flesh.

The poor book had been destroyed by water seeping in from somewhere, but from where? Suddenly, Joanna felt almost psychotic fear. Something had entered the house, violated her perfect home. How could this happen? The house was sealed; the house was perfect; the house did not allow such things to happen.

As she drew the book out further still from the shelf, it fell apart, its thin pages sullied. She could not hold the smelly slimy thing, and it tumbled glue-less to the floor, dead.

Horrified, Joanna stared down at the lifeless heap of mush staining the floor, but then cast her eyes over the rest of the books on the shelf. They were all infected with what for her felt like the same crime - all sodden - all now blurs of stinking, mindless paper.

Joanna cleared away more contaminated books until the back of the shelf revealed a small crack in the wall, through which water trickled unstoppable.

Joanna could see clearly now that water had dripped

slow but sure onto the book, until it had soaked it up, absorbing as much as it could - and then it had simply given way, rotten. The water, however, had not stopped there. It had continued, regardless, polluting everything in its path,

Joanna was outraged.

Her next reaction, apart from recoiling in disgust, was to try and stop the flow. She quickly determined to fill this crack and let no more water or any other intrusion enter. However, just before her decision became a law, emerging from the crack, squeezing through unexpectedly, there was a sudden and miraculous breath of air, a tiny pulse, something new, yet ancient, and with it everything changed.

This new 'thing', this new intruder, had travelled with the water from what Joanna could only surmise was 'the outside.' Shocked, Joanna breathed in the scent. And it was good.

As much as the water destroying her books had disgusted her, the scent from outside bewitched her and entranced her all at once.

Joanna had smelt nothing like it before. She found herself suspended in time, and space. It was a weird, magical moment, an aroma of perfumes, delicate yet insistent, reminding her of childhood, of primal desires and the most powerful forms of goodness.

It was a transformative moment. Joanna's mouth slowly opened, her nostrils, flared and her heart, so long alone, cracked open a little, too. She gasped. It was all she could do to stay upright on her stool. This smell, this scent, this something strange and different, was from outside and a curious invitation to unpick her whole life and her beliefs.

Joanna was not only flooded with sensation but

also with insatiable curiosity. It was from 'outside,' from beyond the door, where all things 'outside' were considered dangerous. Her heart pounded. The House had warned her, indoctrinated her against it. And yet, here she was, trapped and enslaved by the slightest of scents.

As she got off the stool, Joanna knew what she would do. It was inevitable. She would be unable to fight it; it was something she had t d.

THREE

Of course, Joanna knew where the door to the outside was, even though she had avoided it all her life. The door, a simple thin thing, was on the opposite side of the house, down a long, narrow passage, which twisted slightly and then turned awkwardly, as if it wished to remain secret. With the scent of the alien air still in her lungs she ran towards it, helter-skelter, chaotically bumping into things as she went, but stopping at least three times to gather strength as fear gripped her the closer she got.

Before she knew what was happening, there it was, right in front of her. The door. *The Door*. It was the only object between her and the outside. And yet the air in her lungs still held the remnants of that so small scent, that alluring and oh so exquisite perfume that had captivated and intoxicated her head.

Remembering when she first touched that squelching book, Joanna lifted her hand, extending her fingers to touch the door itself, almost frightened that it, too, would be wet. The door was made of metal, however, and it was hard and solid, but shockingly hot. She flinched - another puzzle in this day of puzzles.

Joanna had been expecting locks, many of them in fact,

but there was only one and its key was in the keyhole itself. Nothing could have been easier. Just turn the key and open the door!

And yet, this was no easy moment. So, Joanna paused. Was the thing she was about to do 'right'? All her life, the House had warned her about 'the outside', all her life she had been 'inside' to protect her from the horrors and the suffering that the outside seemed to offer. What she was about to do seemed madness and yet here she was racing headlong into the utter folly of the unknown.

Every fibre in her body yearned to turn the key, and every bone in her body rebelled against it. Since the library catastrophe, there had been a battle going on inside of her, titanic and subterranean, and the emotional waves, a tsunami of feeling, was only now hitting her shores. Her fingers trembled, her heart beat wild, and her eyes focused on the key, a small golden thing half hidden in a small, dark hole.

Joanna stood there, a monument, living a moment of time stretching into eternity. She was unable to move. Somehow, against all odds, a decision was made and she reached out. Joanna turned the key, and the door opened silently, in slow motion.

The instant she opened the door, she was hit, like a slap, by the heat and the light: solid and sheer they were uncompromising and all-powerful. Joanna gasped and instinctively recoiled, lifting her hands to shield her face as the blinding light needled into her brain and sweat instantly began to pearl on her pale round face.

Unable to escape the intensity of the outside, her knees buckled as if commanded to submit to a cruel master. For the first time in her life, Joanna felt utterly exposed, utterly vulnerable. Here, on the outside, Joanna controlled nothing, owned nothing, was nothing!

And yet, even while these crazed thoughts passed through her head, she felt her body adjusting, acclimatising. Joanna got up. Either the outside had let her go, or she had let go of the inside. Joanna tentatively took her hands away from her face, gingerly uncurling her fingers until she could see what the outside looked like and she unconsciously unbuttoned the top of her dress.

There were steps to the Outside: narrow, steep and long. It was as if she were in an exotic deep well, directly pointed at by the mid-day sun – an agony of purpose exposed. She climbed the steps as if in pain, or on some strange sadistic pilgrimage.

At the top of the unbrushed, unused steps, what she saw before her took her breath away; it was beautiful beyond description. Here was Nature at its most glorious, its most provocative, its most mysterious! Joanna saw no endings and no beginnings, the tangled complexity of chaos and energy, the smashed up crash of life's interminable struggle, of unceasing survival.

Joanna wept as she felt the novelty of being humbled by something greater than herself, but more than anything, Joanna *felt* and her heart cracked open a little more.

In the distance was a huge mass of undifferentiated green where individual trees seemed to merge and fuse together into an endless wood or forest, stretching like a borderless whole as far as her eyes could see.

But in front of her, right there at her feet, Joanna lived the shock of a riot of multi-coloured flowers, on fragile stems, pestered and enjoyed by countless insects: flying, climbing, feeding, fighting. They all had their reasons, their patterns, their sounds, but above everything else, Joanna heard the drone and buzz of laden bees.

The sight and sound and smell of all this newness amazed Joanna. And something deep inside her realised something essential. This was life, real life, living, breathing life: abundant, unfettered, controlled by nothing but instinct and chance.

And now she knew what the scent in the library was and where it came from, what it meant. And the library had just been a hint, not this full-scale, engulfing attack. Joanna sat down as she felt she might fall or faint. She no longer knew the difference between agony and bliss. And then Joanna faltered. It was all too much! She collapsed onto the hard summer ground and cursed the House. Why had all this beauty been kept from her? Why had her parents hidden her away like this? Why the lack of imagination that had limited her life? Why the waste?

Rage suddenly burst from her, hot and keen, filling her every pore, and her every cell. She screamed, long and loud, purging something deep inside, releasing her anger that her life had been stolen from her: a robbery, premeditated, unforgiveable and cruel, a song from a different age.

No one heard her scream save a few scattering birds.

And then, silence. The 'outside' was as indifferent as her parents. A cloud unexpectantly went in front of the sun and everything, all the wonder and experimentation, seemed diminished and cheap. Joanna sobbed. Why had she been deprived of all this? Why?

And then the sneezing began, an explosive unbroken chain of sneezes, beyond control, beyond comprehension.

FOUR

Joanna panicked. She had no idea what was happening to her. So, she fled to the safety of her House, slamming the thin metal door behind her, heart racing, eyes stinging and nose running. Too late she hoped to force the outside, to keep its distance. But the dam was broken and the midday madness complete.

Even inside the sneezing did not stop; sneeze after sneeze after sneeze ripped through her body and shook her to her core. Was this what it was like to be ill, she thought? How long would it last? What was to become of her?

Still shocked, the scents and smells and the memories of what she had experienced were all around her; they penetrated her clothes, replacing the clinical, clean smells of the interior. She stripped and showered, but still they continued. She felt humiliated. It was as if the 'outside' had given her a massive kick for having ignored it so long. Revenge?

Control was what she needed right now, Joanna concluded; so she resolutely returned to the library with her symptoms and sat down to do some level-headed research.

Imagine her delight - and relief - when she understood that hers was a natural reaction to being exposed to light and pollen and the newness of everything in the natural air around her! Further, a simple anti-histamine tablet could solve the problem. Joanna ran to the medical room, grinning smugly.

Joanna strangely felt more proud of herself than she had ever done before. She had not only gone outside, but also controlled it, and conquered it as well – absolutely everything it had thrown at her!

With this success, Joanna agreed with herself that she would definitely go out into the outside world again … but not quite yet. Cautious of becoming ill again, Joanna therefore stayed inside for next few weeks, researching every disease – its causes and cures - mainly in the library, with its nagging reminder still slowly pooling on the floor. However, trying to resume her normal life in the House was impossible. Her outing had been a turning point and there was no going back because the House could no longer contain her.

Over time, Joanna became more and more restless and there was an ever growing niggle at the back of her brain and in the hidden pit of her stomach. And then there was The House itself! Nothing was the same; The House was being spoiled and slowly ruined in front of her eyes. And, for the first time, she felt how awful loneliness is.

But rather than being decisive, Joanna experienced once more, the push-me-pull-you emotions overwhelming her, freezing her now between hope and despair. Thus paralysed, Joanna bypassed the heat and light of summer while autumn, with its altogether different rhythm and passion, established itself in the great outside.

FIVE

Joanna's yearning finally overpowered her fear. She confidently dowsed herself with powders and pills and, shortly after tea, ventured outside once more. She wore looser clothes than normal because she was expecting stifling heat and eviscerating light. But, at the top of the steps, she was greeted by a mellowing sun and a hidden chill. Thankful, she took in the view. How changed! How different!

Gone were the greens and the flowers, gone the calm and the illusion of order in the oppressive heaviness of summer. Instead, Joanna experienced a dizzying array of reds and golds, of browns and yellows, clashing and clambering, yet all in irresistible harmony, an altogether different beauty. In this landscape, every tree was different and distinct, their individuality triumphant and obvious.

Joanna stood and stared, mesmerised. No amount of reading could have prepared her for this grandeur, this bountiful jumble of colour, horizon-bound.

After the shock of summer, this was the most wonderful thing she had ever seen in her life.

In the place of the carefree riot of colourful flowers, were dry old stalks full of seeds, and in their wake and servitude, a thousand tiny birds, competing, flicking and fluttering around the old plants, picking and circling and chattering performing acrobatics in these last few weeks of plenty.

And when a breeze came out of nowhere, Joanna heard the trees crisp and cough, crackling a long dry old rattle, over and over, and saw starlings rising in their cloudy thousands, mad chattering, to circle and sweep in the clear blue sky, while heavy crows hopped clumsily in small black groups, cawing, cawing, cawing. Joanna had never seen so many animals, so completely indifferent to her, so unaware of her presence. Once again, she felt humbled.

However, the smell of decay was not so new to her. She had smelled a hint of it before – once – mingled and merged with so many others, in the library on that fateful day, the old odour of life at the edge. She had sensed that back in the library. But here, in the great outside, it was richer and more potent and strangely more alive.

Joanna absent-mindedly walked around the structure that was her home, the outside of her house, noticing the extent to which it was mostly below ground, like a dungeon. This was her home, a low structure, coming out of the soil like a monstrous mushroom. It was mostly buried, and hidden, with only the top metre, poking out, rounded and colourless, the roof, over shooting the dirty grey walls by maybe another metre.

Despite its form, the House looked alien here. It did not fit into the environment, but seemed stranded rather or hopelessly stuck in the surrounding mud. Here and there, on the unlikely roof, there were colonies of withered grass and straggling weeds. They looked worn and old and Joanna reflected sadly that she, too, was aging. Only this morning

Cracks, Doors, Windows and a Story-Telling Tree

she had found an unexpected white hair flaunting itself in her fringe.

Exploring the huge circumference of the House, Joanna, also noticed that further off, a mossy old log had snagged on a rock and tangled itself in the river bank, immoveable, creating a dam of water behind it, which spilled and spewed to create a small, new channel directed at the House. She had found the cause for the crack in the wall, the reason why she was standing here at all!

For a slight second, Joanna felt that rage swell up again at the water's temerity, its audacity, its outrageous quest to destroy her House, but she crushed her emotions and focused on saving the House, its contents, its silent being, its security.

Joanna turned from the House and thought about what she had to do to solve her problem. She rolled up her sleeves, relishing the thought of repairing the House and returning it to its pristine state.

She found herself marching over to the place where the water was flooding and she knew how easy it would be to stop it up and block it from ever happening again. A few heavy stones would do the trick for now, but a permanent solution would have to wait a little longer.

Joanna pulled the log out of its mire and, unintentionally burst a few buttons on her pastel blouse. She then placed several large rocks at the mouth of the channel, which then soon began drying up, wasting away and shrivelling into the boggy ground, consumed.

Joanna looked down at her handiwork and once more felt that up swelling of parental pride, that is until she noticed the muddy ground squirming with life, wriggling, trying to escape and survive in the drying air.

Joanna, deeply alarmed, immediately cupped the tiny creatures and carried them back into the life-giving waters of the stream, where large fish raced to gorge on the unexpected treats. Shocked, Joanna realised that there were consequences to actions, even hers, and that here there were no judgements, no crime, no punishment. Here was life as it has always been, plain and simple, a beautiful battlefield.

Suddenly exhausted, Joanna retreated into the safety and warmth of The House and she decided that next time she went out, she would be ready and properly prepared.

SIX

Safe inside the House, Joanna promised herself to think honestly about the outside, her mind dwelling especially on the slight creatures, which had wriggled and squirmed in her helping hands, only to be eaten in the filling stream, by bigger and faster fish. In saving her home, she had inadvertently destroyed *their*s and she felt incredibly pained by guilt. That she could ever be the cause of such suffering disgusted her. And yet, was she truly to blame? Wasn't it the log's fault that a channel was forged; the water's fault that had seeped into her home? But then, would she have ever left the House and experienced the outside but for the crack in the wall, the water, the log, the stream…?

Joanna's mind circled and puzzled with blame and fault for hours. Round and round dizzied the arguments, further and further back, where chance happenings had led to unpredictable outcomes, actions with unknowable consequences.

Eventually, Joanna could only conclude that change was inevitable, welcome even, and the crack in the wall became a beginning and an ending, a question and answer all rolled into one, a place of no blame and a place of no ulterior meaning.

No wonder it was a good two months before Joanna felt the urge to go outside again. But as dusk approached one nameless evening, her mind turned to another outing, no fear, no doubt. She dressed for the powerless sun with a long, warm coat, a free-flowing scarf and a cap, which would not hold her hair in place; no matter how hard she tried.

This time, on the outside, an eerie stillness greeted Joanna, a palpable, pressing silence, the heavy silence of snow piled on snow, a smothering snow, lying smug and on top of all life, chilling and killing with exquisite beauty and extraordinary impartiality. Here was Death as a beautiful still life, devoid of breath and devoid of movement.

Near her feet, where the snow seemed less thick, she saw a small bird, dusted with new snow. It was dead. Stiff. Back arched in rictus or pain, she did not know which. This, then, was death, right in front of her, part of her landscape, part of her. Joanna did not know why it had died – old age, starvation, the cold, any number of things, she supposed. But there it was.

Joanna held its tiny frame for what seemed like an age in which she and the universe froze, but eventually she let it slide onto the ground once more, like a piece of discarded cardboard, a perfect simulacrum of life.

Joanna felt that death very keenly. She had never seen death before. Never knew it till now, and so close and so intimate. Even her parents had simply blinked out of her existence, turning themselves off like one of her computers, leaving no trace other than the House itself.

Joanna glanced over to the woods where the trees wore their winter armour: skeletal trunks and branches. She seemed surrounded by death now; she saw its bleakness

Cracks, Doors, Windows and a Story-Telling Tree

everywhere and her heart slowed and was about to be taken over by grief when she noticed that amongst the wet blackness of the trees was also green - the living lichen, the moss, the algae. And suddenly, an owl, outstretched swooping, obeying its own laws, flew in utter silence, with a small vole limp in its beak.

And so Joanna reimagined death, death as necessary, death as part of life itself. Here, death was a priority just as much as life was. Life was still beating though hidden, deep below or deep inside. And Joanna rejoiced in the fact that even here in the midst of winter, life survived and even thrived.

Joanna suddenly burned with a single clear thought: her House had been this snow, had enfolded her, had kept her dead to the world. But another thought pushed its way through her anger and reminded her of where she was – outside!

Joanna stopped, confused, overwhelmed as something new was bursting inside her, something filtering through bone and skin.

And that is when Joanna birthed her great idea, her grand design.

SEVEN

In the past, the House had served Joanna well, but now she felt she needed more. Over the long, dark winter months Joanna drew up plans to alter the House, and patiently waited for the weather to improve, so she could start.

Meanwhile, Joanna did what preparation she could on the inside. First, she tidied the library until it was an empty space, cleared and clean. Then, she outlined in chalk where a new door to the outside world would go, and readied the resources she needed.

With the weather getting warmer and lighter daily, the dawn that Joanna had been waiting for soon broke and out she went.

Outside, Joanna was greeted with the outrageous outburst chorus of birds singing, loud and egregious; nothing held back. To Joanna, the song's power was more than just birds claiming territory or making mating calls. Humans had evolved with these sounds and they immersed Joanna's heart with something primal, something totally absent in the still quiet and calm in the House. The strength of these sounds finally breached her lonely heart and broke into the bond she had with her House and joined it.

Joanna's idea was to excavate deep down till she came to

the level of the floor in the library, clearing a huge space in front so she could build a patio and a grand flight of steps, spreading up slowly in wide semi-circular arcs, fanning out and up to ground level, where Joanna would plant a garden, which, in turn, would wander as far as, and into, the woods beyond.

When Joanna dug down now, she dug out her House with joy not guilt. And as she dug, birds flocked to her; they spied the worms and larvae, bugs and grubs that she was unearthing, re-establishing an ancient partnership. Joanna was entranced that she was helping the birds, their mouths crammed with food and she at once understood the auld alliance, and her heart sang, too.

Joanna had set herself a huge task, but spring both invigorated and inspired her. She worked on the House in the mornings, devoted herself to walking in the woods and creating a garden in the afternoons. But every night she returned to her nest, her safety and her security.

So, Joanna tore down the old cracked library wall replacing it with huge French windows, open to air and sky, letting in the light of the seasons and the heat of the day, and the cold turning stars at night. And so the outside was invited to come inside and stay.

Nevertheless, Joanna built a secondary pair of doors, on rollers, just behind the French windows, so that when brought into position, the House was sealed off and secure once more.

Joanna had her past, and now she had her present, like a jigsaw, which fitted rather marvellously together. However, in *her* jigsaw there were no edges or endings, no straight lines and no precision corners. For this jigsaw, new pieces were continuously added, increasing in size and shape, in depth and in splendour, on and on, and on and on.

The boundless woods slowly merged with the garden, and the garden stretched itself in effortless cascades down the steps that Joanna had made, where they mingled joyously with the potted plants on the patio below.

The House had long ago embraced Joanna, but now the outside embraced her, too. She was part of both, and Joanna embraced them both; and the seasons and cycles, the subtleties of time and place cogged themselves together and span themselves into gold.

The crack in the wall had grown into a door; Joanna was no longer an orphan and all she needed to do, was to maintain her Home and do the Garden.

IGOR'S MONSTER

DEDICATION

This little story is dedicated to Chris G, a good friend and a brilliant teacher, and much, much more.

ONE

When the alarm went off, Igor, a confirmed bachelor, who had long ago controlled his passion, locked away his spirit and pacified his soul, was already awake because his body already knew what time it was through long, relentless training. Igor, therefore, got up and minutely followed his everyday routines, finding himself, forty minutes later, double-locking his rock-like front door, all crisp and clean, and gratifyingly on time.

Igor was irritated when he noticed the garden gate was ajar. He arched his eye-brows as he remembered only too clearly his well-buttoned parent's chorusing, "People who left doors open - or windows or gates - were born in a barn; no manners!" He squared his shoulders, straightened his hat, and brushed an invisible mark from his coat.

Having gone through the metal gate, he turned to close it, raising the latch and hearing the slight unwelcome creak of age and rust. It was then, out of the corner of his eye, that he noticed something else, which was out of place and strange.

Startled, the gate remained unclosed. For there, standing three metres tall, all hair and lumps, and fanged and clawed, one paw outstretched, and the other covering its over-large chest, was what can only be described as a monster, the unwanted stuff of childhood.

Igor did what any one of us would have done; he blinked the creature out of his mind, and scuttled away. A few metres down the road, however, Igor bravely looked back, in order to convince himself that he had not seen anything of the sort, and was rewarded with the blank bland nothingness that he so desperately wanted.

Unwilling to retrace his steps to close his gate, Igor walked briskly onto work and by the end of the day remembered nothing of his encounter, having successfully dismissed the wayward vision entirely from his mind.

TWO

The following morning, surprisingly, the alarm woke Igor! Getting up in a panic, Igor double-locked his front door only slightly later than usual.

It was this act, this ritual locking of the front door, which unfortunately triggered the memory of the 'sighting' from the previous morning. And, having his back to the garden gate, this also made him somewhat apprehensive. "What if that thing were there again?" he thought, slowly allowing his eyes, like small twin skaters, to roll to their corners without moving his head.

To his great, great horror, Igor saw the Monster standing bigger than before, hairier than before, with claws larger and fangs sharper than before. It was indeed real, and just inside the garden gate. It stood, one hand still outstretched, and the other holding against its out-bursting chest, something beating, something scaring, something altogether alien, while its cavernous mouth made a sound very much like, 'let me in'.

Igor unlocked his door as quickly as his small, shaking hands permitted and slammed it shut after he had all but fallen inside, safe at last!

His heart pounding for the first time in years, Igor made

sure that the front door was secured before doing anything else.

After his second sugarless tea, Igor felt strong enough to phone in sick. It was obvious he was not well. Overwork probably. Feverish maybe. Certainly agitated beyond reason. But Igor did not contact the doctor. He did not wish to bother him over such a personal affair, and besides, he was brought up to fight his own battles, to endure and to never give in. So, Igor took himself to bed and slept fitfully for a change, dreaming of melting doors, open gates and broken locks.

Igor, still in pyjamas, walked slowly to the front door and dared himself to look through the door's round, little peep hole, a tiny window onto the weirding world of the outside, to see if he could glimpse the Monster at the gate.

To Igor's great, great horror, the Monster's searching eye looked back, their pupils, black pits of unrequited emptiness, and through the wood the Monster's urgent voice was plain and pleading. For an eternal second, both creatures stared at each other, stunned, before Igor fled back to the safety of his bed and his newfound dreams.

THREE

Sometime in the afternoon, Igor heard the front door open, close, and then the soft swish of a cheap, synthetic coat being taken off. The cleaning lady had arrived.

Mary Daily was a good, honest, middle-aged woman, who had no children, but a husband who was sick, long-term and incurable, which was why she cleaned for people, and how she earned enough to keep her dignity and her house. She was also a small, pious woman, whose busy knees had polished the step of many an altar rail.

Igor was frightened that Mrs Daily might have inadvertently let 'him' in, so he called out:

"Mrs Daily?" his voice just loud enough for her to hear from downstairs.

"Oh, Mr Hide I didn't know you was here," she replied. There was surprise in her voice, but there was also sunshine, as if she were glad he was there, because she liked company and was now eager for some conversation.

Unfortunately for Mrs Daily, the employee and employer rarely met. She was paid by cheque left neatly on the Formica kitchen table (easily cleaned) at the end of every month, without fail.

"Well, I am here; yes! Did you notice anything as you came in?" asked Igor, trying not to sound anxious.

"Excuse me?" she answered. She had not understood. But then, who would?

Igor repeated his question, but this time her answer was closer. She was coming up the stairs! She felt concerned but also nosey.

"Are you alright, Mr Hide? No work for you today?"

"Yes, I mean no, bit of a fever. Please don't come in!" He tried to make himself sound calm. He knew the word 'fever' would have the desired affect and Mary's hallowed steps came no nearer. She had a sick husband to protect after all.

"No, there was nothing outside," Mrs Daily continued, her voice now more worried for her husband than her boss. "No Parcel! Was you waiting for a delivery? I could go to the post office for you if you want. But there's no little red card, like they usually leave."

"No, its nothing like that at all….its just… Nothing. I'm not feeling very well and do not wish to be disturbed!"

"Oh all right, dear…Shall I make you some nice soup then? Leave it in the fridge for you for later?" Her voice went up in tone as she asked the nice questions, expecting a positive response because she was, after all, attuned to the sick, an expert in the needy.

"That would be very kind," said Igor, touched, and suddenly feeling very hungry. He also realised that because Mrs Daily had not noticed anything peculiar as she came in, the Monster must have gone away. Igor immediately felt better and resolved to go downstairs the minute Mrs Daily left.

FOUR

Igor did not go downstairs when Mrs Daily put on her coat, made herself look respectable in the mirror and let herself out by the front door, for he was sound asleep. This time, Igor dreamt of Mrs Daily letting the Monster in, of chicken soup, and of seeing the Monster's probing eyes, not his, reflected in the mirror in the hall.

The alarm did not waken Igor; it was his heart, his strangely beating heart. He sat up, straight-backed, suddenly serious, reviewing his dreams and the whole crazy nightmare of the last few hours and indeed the whole crazy nightmare of the last few days.

All of a sudden, outside of the bedroom quiet, Igor heard a faint, troubling noise coming from downstairs.

"Was Mrs Daily still here?" he thought. "Not possible! I don't pay her to stay *that* long!"

He considered calling the police, but decided to sort it out himself.

Creeping downstairs, Igor felt invisible – and invulnerable - as the thick carpets everywhere absorbed every sound he made, which in turn made the sounds coming from the kitchen all the more jarring and intrusive.

As Igor drew nearer, he discovered, to his amazement,

the Monster – as if he owned the place - sitting at *his* table, sitting on *his* chair, breaking bread and spooning *his* hot chicken soup into what seemed like a very large, starved mouth.

Igor did not know how the Monster knew that he was standing flabbergasted in the doorway, but he turned, without warning, stood up too quickly, and knocked over the table and chair, sending everything crashing violently to the floor, all previous balance broken, all calm destroyed.

Again, there was a moment of sheet-white alarm, an emblazoned second of shocked stillness, the keen intensity of awareness. Igor turned on his heels and ran, like an animal possessed, in total abandonment, back to his bedroom, back to bed, back to where he could cover his head with his bedclothes, and promptly fell asleep.

FIVE

Slowly, and with no hint of sound, the Monster inched out from under Igor's bed. He carefully stood up to his great shielding height, stretched out his enormous limbs - thereby somehow breaking Igor's clock - then brushed, with his small, soft hands, some tiny, stray feathers from his unblemished frame, and allowed a massive smile to slowly spread across his downy face.

"Peace at last!" he thought, and he slipped between the sheets, careful not to disturb the sleeping man, as his weight pressed down on the mattress beside him.

A sigh came from that bed then, a deep, deep sigh, and the Monster, tired beyond imagining, cuddled up to Igor with the gentleness only a Mother could know, and the tenderness only a Father could show.

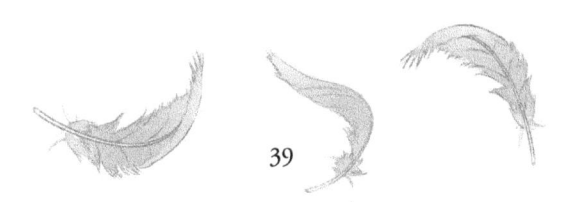

SIX

When Igor awoke, he felt alive and outlandishly happy. He blinked, yawned, but then snuggled back down into the warmth of his bed and enjoyed an extra few minutes of peace.

Eventually, Igor arose, and he opened all the windows in the house, rolled back all the doors, and allowed in the most beautiful of days...

THE STORY-TELLING TREE

DEDICATION

This short story is dedicated John, the best of friends!

ACKNOWLEDGEMENTS

I acknowledge my debt to Siddharta, Candide and, curiously enough, in hindsight, Pogle's Wood, a popular British children's TV show in 1960s (my favourite anyway).

ONE

When we moved into our new house, the first thing I noticed was the tree at the bottom of the garden; it was huge and its branches spread so high that they seemed to hold up the sky itself, while the gripping roots, thick-grained and tough, plunged down into the deep Earth, where no light is, and no wind. The tree's trunk was so broad and massive that my out-stretched arms were unable to encircle it. It was only when Mum, Dad and my little sister and me came together that we were able to properly reach all the way around it – and then only with our fingertips touching!

The tree at the bottom of the garden! 'Tree' – such a small word for something, a living thing, so vast.

My Dad said that a tree that big must be very old indeed. He said that it must have been old during the World Wars; old when Queen Victoria was young; old perhaps, when Columbus discovered America.

Mum said that if a tree that old could talk; it could certainly teach us all a thing or two!

With my mother's words fading, something strange started happening. First, came the goose pimples on my arms, legs, everywhere. Then, a funny feeling in the pit of my stomach, which eventually made my head tingle. Finally, I felt my hair stand on end.

Magic.

Magic was obviously in the air, but it seemed that only I was feeling it. The rest of my family were just as they always were.

Only I was feeling the magic because, at that particular moment, only I was touching the tree!

"What will happen next?" I asked myself, half in fear and half in expectation. Maybe it would only be a matter of time before something wonderful, something truly great would happen – the only thing was… when?!

After that weird experience, I took to regularly sitting under the tree and every day I thought about what had happened after my Mum had said what she had said – the weird feelings, and the hope of magic to come.

And so I waited and waited…and waited and waited. But nothing at all happened. No magic. Nothing. Nothing, that is, except Nature's extra-ordinary 'magic', the greatest magic and the best. And how beautiful was the seasonal magic performed on the tree at the bottom of our garden:

In Spring there were scented flowers on its branches;

In Summer there was cool shade beneath it;

In Autumn there was fruit;

And in Winter I could feel the still beauty beneath the waiting boughs and the pulsing life beneath the layers of indifferent snow.

By now, of course, I had been waiting so long for any kind of magic that I was starting to think that nothing would happen, that I had made the whole thing up, imagined the

Cracks, Doors, Windows and a Story-Telling Tree

weirdness, when, suddenly, out of the blue, something did actually happen.

And this is how it all began:

An ant, one tiny, courageous and determined little ant, was passing right by me on its way up the tree, followed, a few seconds later, hot on its trail, by a few more little ants, all tiny, all courageous, all determined. Where they were going, I did not know. Why they did what they did, I did not know.

I did not know and yet I felt that, for the first time in my life, I really did want to know! You see, I usually ignored things like that, but luckily that day I did not. That day I stopped thinking about myself for a while, stopped thinking about the tree for a while, stopped thinking for a while about the magic that I desperately wanted to happen, and began to watch the world around me in those ever so small scurrying creatures. I was fascinated. I studied them and became totally engrossed in the struggle of their tiny, little lives.

Watching the ants, I had entirely forgotten about the tree, entirely forgotten about the magic, and entirely forgotten about myself.

And that was exactly when the magic happened again.

I heard a voice.

It was not an ordinary voice.

It was a magical voice, deep, sonorous, warm and kind. A voice like a voice belonging to someone you have always loved. It was a voice which rumbled and boomed in a quiet, pleasant kind of way. It was a voice which had all the time in the world. A voice which savoured every word and wasted none. A voice which knew life, a voice which celebrated being alive. A Real Friend's voice!

But it was also a commanding voice, a voice of authority, a voice which knew exactly what it was talking about. And the sound of that voice rolled on through my body so that every cell, every fibre and every nerve vibrated to every single word which was being said.

This was magic – real magic.

And I knew without a shadow of a doubt that it was that old tree's voice, a voice from the bottom of the garden.

Don't ask me how I knew, I just did!

"Hmpf…," said the tree, "those ants, our little sisters, are so interesting, aren't they?"

"Yes," I replied, not really knowing what to say.

"And I suppose you were wondering just what exactly they're doing, and why…" said the tree.

"Er…y-es," I managed to stutter, wondering just how the tree knew what I was thinking.

Magic.

"Well," said the tree, "I like an inquisitive mind, a mind which is open to more things than just itself! And as you seem so fascinated by our little sisters, I could tell you all about them, if you wanted me to. Would you like me to tell you the story of the ant?"

"Yes, I mean, yes please! I would very much like to hear the story of the ant!" I said as calmly and as politely as I possible could, looking at the tree, but not quite knowing where to look exactly. Well it's not everyday that a tree wants to tell you a story, is it?

"Good," replied the tree, sounding very satisfied, "very good. I like that. I like someone who knows what he wants

Cracks, Doors, Windows and a Story-Telling Tree

and keeps it short. Not like some birds I know…they can chatter on for an age without really saying anything, you know…but then who can blame them?" asked the tree with a smile in its voice, "they speak so beautifully. And after all, chattering along is their nature, the way they were made to be…By the way, you'd better make yourself comfortable, the story of the ant is a long one. Ants go a long way back…"

So after I had settled down, and got myself comfortable in a leafy nook between two jutting roots covered in moss, the tree began telling me the long, curious story of the ant.

"Yes; ants go a long way back…" laughed the tree. "Did you know that ants were on this Earth long, long before your kind were even imagined?"

"Really?" I asked, incredulously. It seemed to me that people had always been. I could not really imagine a world without people.

"Yes," answered the tree, "hundreds of millions of years ago ants were caught in amber. Er…do you know what amber is?" asked the tree.

"No," I answered. I was beginning to feel rather foolish and ignorant.

"No need to be embarrassed little brother," said the tree, kindly, "learning and growing are fine things. It's those who stop learning and growing who should be embarrassed, you know…it's those who stop learning and growing who cause most of the problems…but that's another story…Hmpf…but let's get back to 'amber' shall we? Well…what we trees call fossilised 'tree juice' you humans call 'amber'…and ants – and all kinds of other small creatures, for that matter – sometimes get caught up in it, that is, if they're unlucky enough…it begins its life as very sticky stuff, you see, thick as syrup when it's wet, and hard as stone when it's dry…and once those tiny tangled up creatures get completely covered over with it, they are preserved inside for all time, in every last detail…but then," laughed the tree, "that's yet another story, isn't it? We really must not get off the track of the story of the ant or we'll be here forever. You see, every story is joined onto every other story, just like everything is joined onto everything else! And it is so easy to get side-tracked. It's all one big story really…."

Right there and then, I found what the tree had just said very hard to understand. What did it mean, everything was part of "one big story"? It just did not make sense. It was only much later that I came to appreciate what the tree was trying to teach me…

Magic.

And so the tree told me the story of the ant – from the very beginning to the very end, well not quite to the end because, the tree explained, "the story of the ant is far from finished. In fact," it explained, "those ants, our little brothers and sisters have still got a lot more living and walking and talking to do on this spinning Earth!...Yes," the tree went on, "the ants have a way to go yet unlike some other little brothers and sisters whose stories were ended before their time… "And a whole world of sadness welled up through the tree's belly-deep voice. "Some stories, however, are sadly finished… Yes; some very good stories, some very good friends are no more, they have been ended…"

The tree had spoken with such sorrow in its voice that I, too, felt my heart sinking, even though I did not really understand what that sadness was all about.

Cracks, Doors, Windows and a Story-Telling Tree

Without warning, the tree sighed, said "Hmpf..." and then plunged straight back into the story of the ant...

And the story of the ant turned out to be every bit as fascinating as the tree had promised. The story of the ant showed me our little sisters as they *really* are: their thoughts, their fears, their hopes; how they feed and how they breed, how the ants helped the tree and how the tree helped them – a thousand things, interesting, useful, secret. But most importantly, perhaps, the story of the ant told me about dependence and interdependence, about how all things are joined to everything else. And while some people called this a chain, or a web, some others gave it no name at all; to them it just *was*.

Magic.

The story of the ant had taken all of that afternoon and some of the evening, too! The tree was right; it was a long story...ants *do* go a long way back!

And when the story was over, the tree fell silent.

Strangely, this silence was neither embarrassing nor oppressive; it was alive and vibrant. For in it were the tree's profound love and understanding. And this impressed me so much that I, too, wanted to love and understand those tiny, courageous, determined little ants in exactly the same way that the tree did.

Magic.

Suddenly, I realised what the time was; it was late. While the tree had been telling me the story of the ant I had not even noticed time passing quietly by.

And if I did not immediately hurry back to the house, my parents would get so worried that they might not allow me to go back there again. So I quickly got up to leave. But before I went, I promised the tree that I would come back the next day. And although the tree remained silent, I knew that it was pleased.

Magic!

Of course, I returned the next day…I wanted more magic, more stories…and while I was getting comfortable again, settling down, hoping that the tree would talk to me like it did the day before, I happened to see a worm trying to ooze its way back into the safety of its hole. It wriggled, expanding and contracting, in pain and fear, desperate to be out of the sun's burning rays and out of reach of any sharp-eyed bird's beak. It suddenly occurred to me that this worm might have a story, like the ant did the day before… and that's when I heard the tree's voice again.

Magic.

"Ha…so you're back!" said the tree, as if talking to an old friend. "Good. Very good. I like that! Its not very often that you get a little brother human being willing to give up its own time to sit and listen. Humans are always so busy doing things. Busy, busy, busy, that's humans! No time to spare, no time to spend, no time for anything but themselves. If only they had time to listen to others instead of just themselves, things might be better…some stories might not have ended so quickly…"

And again there was that penetrating sadness, searing and deep. I, too felt sad again, but this time, I felt different: I really wanted to do something to help, so that this sadness would end – though for the life of me, I could not think what *I* could possible do!

Magic.

"Hmpf…But there we are…" said the tree, "*you're* here

Cracks, Doors, Windows and a Story-Telling Tree

now and for the moment that's all that matters." I was relieved to feel the smile in the tree's voice once again, a smile which lightened all dark corners..."and you've been wondering about that little worm over there, haven't you?"

"Yes," I said, wondering just how it knew so much...

"Would you like me to tell you the story of the worm? It's actually even longer that the story of the ant I told you yesterday! And although it is a much simpler story, it's even more interesting, if that is possible, of course. Yes, worms are very interesting creatures. Very useful, too, don't you know!"

The tree then began another story, the story of the worm.

And as the worm's story unfolded, I was once again amazed at the complexity of it all; how one thing helped another and so on, until *all* life seemed inextricably linked. And it was then that I remembered what the tree had told me the day before – about everything being "one big story." Was I perhaps beginning to understand?

Magic.

And so it went on.

Everyday I sat beneath the tree, and every day the tree told me about whatever plant or animal had happened to catch my eye and interest.

The bushy-tailed foxes, the gossiping birds, the slow moving snails with their mad, moon-shine trails, whizzing insects and even the wind, the rain, and the sun and the moon. Nothing was too big or too small. Everything had a place in the tree's stories.

And little by little, I came to realise that the tree was indeed right – there was only "one big story", a really big one, the incredible story of the Earth! For, just as the tree had said, everything is joined onto everything else, in some way or another.

Magic.

And so it went on.

Until, one day, the tree told me the story of Man, the story of men and women, of children, of the peoples of the world. People like me – my family, my friends.

At first, the tree told me how glorious, how mysterious and how great being human is; it told me of thought and laughter; of tears and love. But then it began to tell me about fire, and houses, about the woodcutter, and the forest burner, the sharp-edged axe and the bitter saw.

But the tree did not stop there; it carried on relentlessly, telling me about oil slicks and nuclear waste, about hate and War.

I felt so ashamed to be human. But sooner than I could have imagined, my feelings quickly slipped into horror and anger and finally hate. The tree reacted to my emotions with the shuddering revulsion, and then suddenly the only emotion I was left with was pity, which thankfully melted into compassion: for the suffering world, and for its People.

And then I realised that I no could longer ignore the things around me, that I had come to love everything that the tree had been telling me about…and I also realised that somehow the People's attitudes, like mine, needed to be changed…and I had to think of a way to stop Stories from ending…

"Little brother," asked the tree, softly, "are you wondering what your role could be in 'the big story'?"

"Yes," I answered humbly.

"It is simple," said the tree with a huge smile in its voice.

Cracks, Doors, Windows and a Story-Telling Tree

"Tell me," I brightened.

"You can tell *me* a story!" It said with hardly a pause.

"A story? Me?"

"Yes, little brother. You can tell *me* a story."

"But I don't know any stories!" I pleaded.

And then the tree laughed! A great roaring deep-down belly-laugh, a laugh to set the whole world to rights, if we would only learn to listen.

"You humans," said the tree, still laughing, "you are so strange! You think you know so much and yet you really know so very little. Humans rarely know their own stories and that is your tragedy, of course. You say you don't know any stories and yet you are living one yourself right now, little brother...what of *your* story? You, who have been listening to me all this time, surely *you* could at least tell me your *own* story?"

"I...don't know," I answered unsure of myself, "I didn't think that my story would be very interesting, I suppose."

"But little brother, the story you tell, will be a unique one."

"Unique? Me?"

"Yes! Unique and Special. It will be special because *you* are our hope, the future's and the present's, the hope of all living things...because *you* can actually do something to change the way your kind thinks and behaves. Most humans have stopped listening to everyone else's stories, you see. They need a fellow human being to teach them to listen once again.

"You can tell them our stories, teach them that they are part of everything, that they, too, are part of the 'one big story'! You see, little brother a time for telling has come.

Tell them that everything follows when they learn to listen, when they learn to love."

"And that, little brother, will be your great task, your own great story."

"It will take a life-time," added the tree, "a whole life-time, little brother."

"And when you have finished your story, little brother, when you are old, creature of the Earth, would you come back here and tell it to me? Would you stretch yourself beneath my limbs and tell me your tale, slowly and in great detail>"

"For I shall be here waiting for you. And I shall listen to you even as you have listened to me."

"And, little brother," said the tree, its voice rich and mellow, "we will learn and grow together. And our stories will be one, little brother...part of that 'one big story'.

And when you have truly finished your story, and you have fallen silent as your slowing heart, it will be time for me to tell you a longer tale and a greater.

For, I will tell you of the strange, great story of the stars..."

TWO

A boy becomes a man so quickly. Too quickly, perhaps. He cannot wait to see the magic that was, slowly turn to tricks and trickery, the gods mere myths and life itself the dream of an endured survival, and nothing more.

The boy had grown into a man now with a wife, young children of his own, a mortgage, a car, debts and a job and it had been very many long years since he had had time to visit his parents and the tree at the bottom of their garden.

But now he was back. Divorced. Redundant. Repossessed. Black-listed. A disappointment. A life in chaos. A life in ruins. The old paths forgotten…the newer obliterated. A failure in the eyes of all but those last two, who loved him unconditionally and would be waiting for him, always, with cups of tea and smiles…

The man's parents were old now, even though he had not seen this ever so slow transformation. For while he had been away, they had grown everyday more like trees: bent and gnarled, ancient and ageless and yet still strong inside. They told him to go into the garden while they, slow-moving, prepared something to eat. "You used to love sitting under that great tree," they said smiling strangely, knowingly. "Perhaps it could teach you a thing or two now…"

L. Peter Jones

The man had long forgotten about the tree; long forgotten about the magic; long forgotten about childhood truths.

With his parent's words fading, something strange started happening. First came the goose pimples on my arms, legs, everywhere. Then, a funny feeling in the pit of my stomach, which eventually made my head tingle. Finally, I felt my hair stand on end.

And then it all came flooding back – all the childhood he had hidden; all the wonderful lessons he had ignored because he had become serious and grown up and busy and head-strong and ambitious, living other peoples' wishes and other peoples' lives, not his own.

And he wept. He wept for what he had lost and missed; wept for what he had once dreamed was possible and had not come true. He wept honestly for the first time in years, remembering what it was like to feel the truth and live it. He sat under the tree, touching it lightly with his fingertips, in trepidation and fear. For what if the magic did not work? Would this be something else that would be denied to him? What if it had been just a childhood dream after all? What if? What if? What if? And yet the man tried. For there was enough of the boy in him yet to try, and that is all he needed.

Magic.

And a great booming voice filled his head.

It was a deep voice, sonorous, warm and kind. A voice like a voice belonging to someone you have always loved. It was a voice which rumbled and boomed in a quiet, pleasant kind of way. It was a voice which had all the time in the world. A voice which savoured every word and wasted none.

Cracks, Doors, Windows and a Story-Telling Tree

A voice which knew life, a voice which celebrated being alive. A Real Friend's voice!

But it was also a commanding voice, a voice of authority, a voice which knew exactly what it was talking about. And the sound of that voice rolled on through the man's body so that every cell, every fibre and every nerve vibrated to every single word which was being said.

"Welcome back little brother," it said.

And the grown man wept again. For something in him which was too tight and brittle had broken and a dam was breached. For this was the very first time that he had believed in himself for a very long time.

"Yes; I'm back," said the man, leaning on the tree, "but my life's a mess; I'm a failure. I've let you and everyone down."

"A failure?" asked the tree taken aback, not a little shocked. "Let me and everyone down?"

"Yes, yes, yes," repeated the man, admitting his faults, taking responsibility, like a hammer smashing onto a nail, and not for the first time. "I wish I hadn't failed anyone – especially you. I regret my life bitterly. If I could only change it…"

"Hmpf," said the tree, thinking aloud. "But you are here. How can you regret the life that has brought you exactly to where you should be?"

And now it was the man's turn to be taken aback.

"What do you mean old friend?" asked the man with a glimmer of hope in his voice.

"You're life, you're whole life, has brought you here, to this moment, this place, this now. Is that not a good thing?" And the tree paused to sense how much his friend had suffered. "All you need now, little brother, is understanding, your loving understanding… Your life is one big story like everyone else's, it needs fitting together with kindness, that's all.

"You don't understand," said the man, collapsing into a whine, "My life…I've suffered so much…"

"Everything suffers. You are not alone. But rather than letting suffering stop you living, allow suffering to teach you how to live," said the tree, full of sympathy. "You can learn from your suffering..."

But the man was too close to his pain, holding on to it too tightly and too afraid to believe the tree.

The tree fell silent and in that silence there was love.

"Let me show you your life so far," said the tree, gently, "and then you can decide about change and failure and all the rest you haven't told me…"

And then something truly amazing happened. The whole tree lit up like an enormous Christmas tree, but incredible - Christmas decorations on an unbelievable scale. On each branch and leaf and twig were hundreds or thousands upon thousands even of shining baubles of light. They were all different colours, every imaginable shade and hue. Some bigger and brighter than others; some were smaller but equally spectacular. It was as if someone had pressed the pause button on a fireworks display at the very moment of explosion, the very moment when everyone gasps. It was the most beautiful thing the man had ever seen, the most wonderful, and the most fascinating.

Magic.

And then, without asking why or how, the man knew

exactly what all the shiny baubles were, what they actually meant.

Magic.

In each sphere of light, each bauble, however large or small, was a memory, an incident, a thought even, a moment of his life, something that had made his life what it was: every decision and every choice. All there. Everything. The good and the bad. From the beginning right up to the now. Everything. Everything. Everything. And the man noted even now new baubles of light forming right up at the top of the tree. And they were golden. Everything was there. Everything. Nothing was hidden. Everything revealed.

And then the tree spoke, "Let us view together your life until you can see the rightness of it. You will see all the causes and all the effects, from the very beginning until now…"

"Thank you, thank you," said the man, clutching the trunk of the tree, his lifeboat, his friend, even though he did not entirely understand the words that the tree had spoken.

And then, to his amazement, the man noticed that one of the largest baubles, a sphere of immense crystalline beauty, was detaching itself from the low branch it was balanced on. It hovered as if nervous and unsure of itself for a few seconds before being directed by the tree to come and lay at the man's feet.

Magic.

It was amazing. A huge pulsing Christmas bauble at one's feet, a delicate translucent orb filled with light close enough to touch.

Magic.

And then the light-filled orb began to spin. It spun slowly at first. But its speed gradually built up until it was a blinding blur of sparkling light that looked as if it were stationary. Then it opened, unpeeling from the top, like a timid flower blooming.

And the man was transfixed again with the wonder of it.

Magic.

As the man had suspected, at the heart of the magic of the sphere was a memory. But this memory was so far into his past that it was no longer something conscious but something new and strange.

Magic.

And then the memory, which had also been on hold, awoke and began to unwind its story. For the man it was like watching T.V. in three-D – only that he was both star and spectator at the same time.

Magic.

And so the man, tremulous, watched the events of so long ago: his birth.

Magic.

The man watched enthralled as his birth unfolded in all its drama. He has seen the detail: the fear, the pain, the wonder and the struggle. He did not understand the significance of everything he had seen and yet he knew that this beginning was truly a beginning. This is where all his own fears and pain had started, all his struggle. But also his strength and his courage. It was as if this event, this one single event had shaped everything that followed.

And then, as quickly as it had started, the flower delicately folded-up its rounding petals and the bauble immediately started spinning once again before it floated back to one of the bottom branches of the tree. And the man was alone. Just the man. And just the tree.

Cracks, Doors, Windows and a Story-Telling Tree

"Take a few moments," said the tree. "Looking at such things always take time…"

The man cried. His tears flowed as they had not flowed in many years, even when his wife left him, when his children left him, when he lost his house and everything in it, when he was alone, before he remembered about his parents. All he could do now was cry and cry and cry. But it felt good and it seemed like the right thing to do.

"Why did you choose *this*?" asked the man, with relief and anger and awe and some understanding, too, all at the same time.

"Because this is where you began, where you first sampled the world and decided what life was like."

"I still don't understand," stammered the man, "I can see a little of how I became who I am because of what happened then, but how can I change it all? How can I be different?"

And then the man, shouted, despair gripping his heart, his fists pounding the tree.

"I want my life to be different. I don't want all that pain and suffering."

"You must choose another memory and then another and another till all becomes clear," said the tree, gently, encouragingly. "Only then will you see the bigger picture…"

"The one big story?" spat the man, collapsing to the ground, his head in his hands.

"Yes!" answered the tree, unafraid.

"Why do you cry?" asked the tree, full of a never-ending compassion.

"I'm crying," said the man, "because I can change

L. Peter Jones

nothing. I've failed again... I cannot change the past. I feel so ashamed..."

"It is certainly true that we cannot change the past," agreed the tree, "but then that is not really why you are here, is it?"

"What do you mean?" said the man, surprised out of his own self-pity.

"As I have already said," announced the tree, "you are here to understand the past, to come to terms with it, not to fight it or repress it. It is only when you can understand your past with compassion and love that you can then go forward...so that your life's task may be properly completed."

"Ah! The *task*," said the man almost derisively, remembering more of his childhood dreams and ambitions. "I remember that you said that I had the task to do – tell people your stories, you said, the stories you used to tell me about plants and animals, when I was young that everyone was really part of 'one big story'. You said that I was to 'tell them that everything follows when they learn to listen, when they learn to love.' And that if I told people these things then things would change. You said that I was 'special', too, and that I should come back here when I was older and tell you all about what I had done – tell you *my* story. Well I am here, aren't I, and I have done nothing. Nothing...you must be disappointed..."

"Like your Father at your birth?" asked the tree wisely...

Startled by the tree's insight, the man realised that the tree was gently prodding him in the right direction. He knew. And yet. Could it be true then about patterning? From birth? Beyond our control? We are who we are!

"But I also said," said the tree, reminding the man that

at least he did not have a selective memory! "that you're task would be finished *at the end*...well the end isn't now, is it? You have only just begun...I didn't say that you wouldn't come back for help and guidance before the task was completed, did I?"

As if he had just been thrown a life jacket again, the man gasped. And then it dawned on the man that what the tree had just told him was really quite obvious...and the man felt even more ashamed than before.

"How you complete your task is for *you* to discover!" said the tree, with as much careful wisdom as it could muster. "But before you can recommence your task there is something *else* that you must learn."

"And what would that be?" asked the man, fearful.

"First you must discover who you *really* are..."

"I know who I am!" said the man with as much self-hatred as he dared show, even after being shown all that the tree had shown him. "I'm a failure...you've shown me...I was born a failure and have grown up into one...and, as you've shown me, I can't change a thing, can I?"

"But you can," said the tree chuckling lightly. He always found it engaging the way humans always misunderstood, to the point of wilfulness, what was really intended...

"But how? How can I change things?" he asked confused.

"Well I'm glad you're asking the right questions, now," said the tree now laughing quite hard, which only made the man feel uncomfortable and not a little angry. "But of course, it's all easier said that done..."

"Well," said the man, "I've never liked guessing games... just tell me straight...How can I change things?!"

"You must retrieve what you have lost – or rather

misplaced," said the tree in all seriousness. "You must look at every single one of these beautiful lights and you must acknowledge them, understand them, accept them lovingly, *as they are*…and then you will be who you were meant to be…"

"It certainly sounds simple," said the man, pretending not to be daunted by the sheer amount of twinkling, shining baubles in front of him.

"It's not simple at all, little brother," said the tree, even more seriously. "It all comes down to this. It's a question of Fear or Love. You can either spend your life in Fear or you can spend your life in Love. Repeat your patterns or remove yourself from them. The choice is yours. If you agree to do this thing, you will need all your courage, all your strength. You will be a crusader, an exceptional man of our times. Believe me, it is not at all a simple thing that I ask of you. But it is a thing that I know you can do – or else I would not ask it of you. If it were easy, little brother, half the world would already be here…"

"So why all this then? I mean why do we have to go through all of this?"

"Why do you put yourselves through all of that? Is that what you want to say? Hmpf?" the tree laughed. "Perhaps you will find out that answer for yourself one day, little brother…but now all I will tell you is this…some things are so painful that we guard them close, we do not want to look at them because we think that they might hurt us – again. This is one of the mind's survival strategies. But it is poison to our lives…"

"So we…I….must look at all of me, my memories…" said the man really asking a question.

Cracks, Doors, Windows and a Story-Telling Tree

"Exactly," said the tree, immensely pleased. "Look in order to Love. You see, with every memory, there's a point of energy that goes with it. With integration, comes understanding, and with understanding comes wisdom and so, and you can go forward in life…"

"And if you don't…you're stuck…Is that what you're saying?"

"Exactly," said the tree again. "You've cracked it, as they say, though I don't really approve of that old phrase…"

"Let me see if I've got this right," continued the man, visibly stronger and brighter. "Life's a bit like a…a…an old fashioned steam train. It can't go anywhere without its coal carriages…and you're saying that when something goes wrong without our lovingly understanding, then it's like we lose a carriage full of coal…when we get it back, *and we can*, we can feed the engine again and it's full steam ahead!"

"I'm proud of you," boomed the tree. "I could not have put it better myself!"

The man knew that if the tree had arms to hug him that's what it would be doing now. And then the man laughed.

"It is exactly as you've explained," said the tree, happy that things were beginning to come clearer for the man, his friend and brother, "you cannot change the past…and there is really not point in thinking that you can…the only thing to do is to understand the past, lovingly and with compassion."

"When do I begin?"

"You began two hours ago," said the tree, "about fifteen minutes after your tea went cold!"

And now the man and the tree were laughing together.

Everything seemed all right and yet they both knew what hard work was ahead of them.

"Sit here a while and think, little brother," rumbled the tree, after their bellies had stopped aching with laughter. "Call up your memories, one by one. Look at them. Understand them. Use them to push your steam engine always and forever onwards and upwards…and then forget about them…and before you know, your task will be complete…"

The man knew he could stay beneath the tree awhile, looking at the beautiful baubles, which only he and the tree could see, learning, for as long as he wished. Time did not matter. He was in control again…and determined to follow the way of the tree until, that is, it was time to leave and go his own way…

So the man sat beneath the tree, his old friend, and for the first time, in a very long time, he saw the stars and a smile spread serenely across his face.

THREE

The man and the tree had found each other long, long ago when he was a child. The tree had told him so many stories about the plants and animals in the world, how everything was interconnected, how everything was really just one big story. The tree also told him that he had a task to accomplish:

'"Most humans," 'the tree had explained to the boy,' "have stopped listening to everyone else's stories…They need a fellow human being to teach them to listen once again. You can tell them our stories, teach them that they are part of everything, that they, too, are a part of the 'one big story'! You see, little brother, a time for telling has come. Tell everyone that everything follows when they learn to listen, when they learn to love. And that, little brother, will be your great story. That will be your task.'"

But as the boy grew up and moved away into adulthood, he shelved his task so completely that he forgot about it until, years later, the man, disillusioned and ruined by the world and the life he had lead, returned to the tree. The tree helped him to remember who he really was, helped him to remember his task and also helped him to remember the strength and courage that he was born with.

L. Peter Jones

The man sat beneath the tree at his parents' house learning and unlearning things for a very long time.

One day, the man said to the tree who had been unusually quiet for a little while, that he was going to pick up all the rubbish that had either been blown or thrown into his parents garden.

"That is good," said the tree in its great booming voice. It was a deep voice, sonorous, warm and kind. A voice like a voice belonging to someone you have always loved. It was a voice which rumbled and boomed in a quiet, pleasant kind of way. It was a voice which had all the time in the world. A voice which savoured every word and wasted none. A voice which knew life, a voice which celebrated being alive. A Real Friend's voice!

But it was also a commanding voice, a voice of authority, a voice which knew exactly what it was talking about. And the sound of that voice rolled on through the man's body so that every cell, every fibre and every nerve vibrated to every single word which was being said.

"Indeed," continued the tree. "Delivering us from rubbish is very good. Many of our little brothers and sisters are killed by human rubbish. They die trapped inside glass bottles that they can't scrabble out of, they are poisoned by the chemicals in some of your foods, they suffocate, they drown, they suffer…"

"Yes, that's exactly what I was thinking," said the man, quietly, full of compassion.

So the man got up from his contemplations and spent the rest of the morning slowly and systematically going round his parents' large garden picking out every last bit of rubbish, however minute.

Cracks, Doors, Windows and a Story-Telling Tree

By the end of the morning, the great, black bin bag, which the man had used to collect the rubbish, was nearly full.

"I never thought our neat garden had this amount of rubbish," he said to the tree, entirely surprised.

"Hmpf," said the tree, thinking aloud. "I know the soil, like I know the plants and the animals. If you think that there is a lot of rubbish here – and your parents are unusual in the care they take of their garden – then just imagine the amount out there, beyond your fence, and all of the tens of thousands of plants and animals suffering and dying because of the things that humans, when they want them no longer, discard so easily, without thought or care.

The next day the man resumed his relearning under the tree but, for the first time since he had come back to the tree, the man felt ill-at-ease. Something was nagging him at the not-too-far-back of his mind.

"What is wrong little brother?" asked the tree, knowing full-well what was wrong.

"I'm not sure," replied the man, shifting his weight. "But ever since I picked up the rubbish yesterday, I have been feeling that something is missing in my life."

"Oh yes?!" said the tree, smiling to itself.

"Yes!" replied the man.

"Tell me more," said the tree interested, still smiling.

The man knew what was coming next. He was going to have to tell a story - the story of his thoughts: full honesty, a searching, penetrating truth.

"You know how much I like sitting here beneath you…" he started.

"It's been a real pleasure for me, too," interrupted the

L. Peter Jones

tree. "Please believe me when I say that I have leaned as much as you…"

"…without you I would not know who I am," insisted the man sincerely.

The tree smiled and that smile was full of love.

"You did it all by yourself, little brother, and I am very proud of you…but you must tell me what is on your mind."

"Well the truth of it is that I feel like I need to *do* something now. I feel like the time to act has come…Perhaps the time for sitting contemplating beneath you is over…

"Well," said the tree, laughing, "sitting is good but doing is better, I suppose. You must do what you must do. Nothing is stopping you. But remember this," continued the tree, knowing that the man was beginning to heal his past hurts and that the man's role was about to change – again, "the time for contemplation is never over. You can act and contemplate at the same time you know. While you act you can contemplate, and while you contemplate you act. Your acts will become contemplations, your contemplations, acts…"

"The only thing is," said the man, listening but still embarrassed, "I'm not sure what I should do…"

"Oh yes you are!" said the tree, teasing. "You just want me to give you a push, that's all!"

The man laughed and then so did the tree.

"OK," said the man. "I've cleaned the garden here, now I feel the need to go 'beyond the fence', as you put it. I'm going to pick up the rubbish in the street. What I will do after that, I do not know but from now on, tree, I will be spending less and less time with you because of this important task I have given myself."

Cracks, Doors, Windows and a Story-Telling Tree

"The task is an important one," said the tree, its great booming voice full of love and compassion. "But don't forget you will always have me close by, I am not only all the plants and all the animals but I am also the soil. Besides, I am in your heart as you are in mine. You could not escape me even if you tried."

"After all," said the man, smiling up at his big brother, "we are all just one great big story, aren't we…?"

And then the man and the tree laughed again. It was good to laugh even though most times now the man and the tree, when they were together, were happy smiling and being quiet with one another. The tree was glad that the man was beginning to remember the important things in life and letting go of the less important things.

The next day, the man started picking up rubbish all around the estate where he and his parents lived. He did not have a plan or a measurable goal. He did not have a timetable. He did what he was doing and it would take as long as it would take, usually as long as the sun let him see.

The man had effectively begun his task. He was wholly present as everything he did was to the fullest expression of who he was. He was helping, being of service, making a difference.

And as he walked unhurriedly picking up rubbish with care and consideration, the man thought about the tree. He thought about *the task:* the one the tree gave him long ago and this his more recent were probably the same, he decided. He smiled. It did not matter really. Whatever he was doing was, he realised, what he should be doing. And that was all he needed to know. It was enough. And the man smiled again, serenely.

Whenever the man saw rubbish he carefully collected it, making sure there were no little animals or plants stuck to it before putting it in his black bin bag. He untangled paper, new or long rotting, he gathered tin-can rings, some still sharp, and was vigilant with broken glass. He soon took to wearing thick gloves.

And then at dusk he would find his way home, putting his bin bags in places he knew the bin men would be collecting the next day, or, better, sometimes, he found a skip and threw the rubbish in.

The bin men were angry with him at first. They thought that he was being paid to clean the streets and so was in some strange way, taking away their livelihood. They lived in Fear. The man ignored their anger. He quietly explained to them what he was doing. They saw his smile. They believed him. They left him alone, thinking he was touched with madness.

When the man finished taking the rubbish from one street, there was always another. The man was not deterred. He was never dismayed either or even hurt to find that the original street would be full of rubbish the day after he had cleaned it.

Eventually, the streets did clear enough so that the man could turn his attention to people's gardens. He knocked on doors and asked politely if he could clean up their gardens for them. He was often met with stunned amazement. But his smile went everywhere with him. He never judged. Sometimes he was met with aggression, and he listened. Most times, however, people said just yes to his request and then, after a while, helped him because they knew he was sincere and they understood what he said. He made people feel valued. He cared.

Cracks, Doors, Windows and a Story-Telling Tree

Basically, the people of the estate, who had known him since he was a child, thought that the man had gone a bit simple or, if they were being kind, eccentric. If that man wants to clean up the estate, which isn't a bad thing, actually, let him; it was time someone did something; if he likes plants and animals – well, who doesn't?

People slowly began to be more careful with their rubbish. They explained to their kids what the man had explained to them how rubbish harmed plants, animals and the soil…and that everyone, after all was said and done, was part of the one big story: when we harm others, we harm ourselves, they said. Of course, there were those who did not give a damn but there were sufficient who listened, that the man made a difference.

From being feared the man became loved. People respected him more and more as they watched. And when their admiration grew sufficiently some of the people coyly emulated…while the man carried on regardless, come rain or shine.

It was around this time that the man's parents died, not long apart, very quietly and peacefully. He followed their wishes, and when he was ready, he sold the house, placing the money in the bank. He was thus free to fulfil his task in the way he felt that would be best.

He said good-bye to the tree before he left.

"Well done," said the tree, immensely proud.

"Thank you…" said the man, reflecting, "…for everything!"

"All I ask is that you don't forget to tell me your story when you're done…!"

"I won't!"

The man smiled. The tree smiled. The stars wheeled and the man walked away without looking back.

FOUR

After weeks of picking up rubbish from the sides of roads, the man noticed an area off the road, partially hidden from view by a thick grove of bushes and trees, a site where a small factory had once been. It had been completely demolished but the whole area had become a magnet for people who used it as a tip. The plants and animals of this whole wasteland area were choked with all manner of household rubbish.

The man said to himself that he was not only going to clear the entire space of rubbish, section by section, but he was also going to plant trees and bushes, flowers and herbs that would attract the animals that were now absent.

The man immediately started clearing the rubbish from the back of the plot so as not to be disturbed, putting all the rubbish near the entrance. Once a small section had been suitably transformed, he bought some forks and spades and dug down to the rubbish beneath the soil.

This completed, the man visited the nearest garden centre. He bought huge bags of compost, lots of buddleia and lady-of-the-forest, and other plants and shrubs, which thrive on poor soil. He also planted hundreds of different types of bulbs. It would soon be spring and he knew that he had a good chance that the plants he had bought would flourish.

In every subsequent section the man repeated exactly what he had done in the first: he cleared it of surface rubbish; he dug the land till it was cleared of buried rubbish; he prepared it for planting; and then he planted it. It took him most of the Spring to clear all of the land in this way. Before finishing up by the entrance to the land, up by the front, where the man had piled all of the rubbish and where people still dumped their rubbish late at night, the man hired several skips. These he quickly filled with all of the accumulated rubbish and then the skips were taken away.

News slowly trickled out that there was a man, maybe even a tramp, working the land on the site of the old shoe factory on the very outskirts of town. There were the taxis, the skips, passers-by. There was a fuss.

The owner of the land was said to be angry. Trespassers were forbidden, after all. The police were informed. Fortunately, the morning the police arrived the man was at the garden centre collecting still more trees, shrubs, ferns and flowers that he had ordered for the final section, the one at the garden entrance. When his taxi drove up, the police had long gone. They had noticed, however, that the place looked much better than it used to.

The garden-factory site soon came to the attention of the local press. A journalist saw a solitary man digging and planting. He was disappointed. He thought he needed eco-warriors and squatters to sell his article. But as he had come all this way he thought he had better interview the man. The man smiled. He was polite. When the other man asked him what he was doing, the man explained clearly and concisely about his task, how he wanted to help the soil and the plants and animals.

Unexpectedly, when the article appeared in the newspaper, a furious debate erupted – for and against the man's task. The journalist was given a bonus. And the newspaper carefully nurtured its new-found goldmine.

Some readers lobbied the local council to protect the new nature reserve. Landowners threatened writs if this were to happen to them. Ordinary people, who also paid their taxes became interested. Perhaps people on the estate, or others around the town, remembered the man and his stories. Ecologists wanted action now before it was too late. The newspaper reported the final opposing positions: bulldoze the New Eden, making way for a brand new factory – with at least new jobs – or preserve, for ever, the whole area as a people's nature reserve…

People from both sides went to see the man but he had already moved on. His task at the new garden was finished and he was already picking up rubbish at another side of another road, walking in his usual slow, unhurried way.

The man knew nothing of the debate. If he found a newspaper on his travels he put it in one of his heavy duty black bin bags. He did not care. It did not matter. He was busy making a difference somewhere else.

And then, as fate would have it, he saw another likely spot to be turned back over to nature. This site was even bigger and more desolate that the old shoe factory. It was now late Summer so he set to cleaning and preparing as he had done in the other place. He would plant what he could.

Unlike the man's first garden, the second was not concealed, and his activities, on the derelict barracks site,

Cracks, Doors, Windows and a Story-Telling Tree

once again came to the attention of the local press. They had been looking for him and were relieved to be able to resurrect the popular and rewarding debate.

The man was not alone for long. A whole band of people just turned up one day. He explained what he was doing. They heard what he was saying but their plans were not his. They wanted to fight the council. The man did not object; he simply carried on doing the garden.

When the police came, a week later, they had been warned to be careful. It was an election year. The press was around. The council wanted to look compassionate yet just. The man carried on, doing what he had always done, in the background, while leaders shouted at leaders. It did not really matter.

The place was cleaned up seeded and planted, so much quicker than the man had thought possible. He was grateful for everyone's help. He said the plants and animals were grateful too. They did not see him leave.

For a short while the man's helpers were somewhat shocked that he had simply upped and left, just when the going was getting tough with the council. But they soon forgot about him; they were busy organising themselves into a group for the protection of another new nature reserve… and managed, with all the publicity and controversy to keep it from being bulldozed and built on. They had public outrage on their side.

While this was happening, the man was busy collecting fallen seeds on the roadside as he walked on. He planted them wherever and whenever he felt it appropriate. He knew some would be eaten, some never germinate, but he did it anyway. He knew the way Nature worked. Something always survived.

The next time the man began clearing a site, another group mysteriously found him and helped him. The man was amazed and grateful as ever. This group seemed better organised from the outset. They had exchanged ideas with the old groups so as to best save the work they were doing.

Little by little, year after year, of transforming every place he passed, completely unknown to him, a nationwide network was being set up. People cleared rubbish even though the man was not there. Debate was no longer local. Parliaments were passing laws because people were putting pressure on them. People were caring more about their environment listening to each other, listening to the stories of the plants and animals and the soil…knowing that we are all just one great big story.

And so, too frail at times to bend to pick up any more rubbish, and most of his work going unnoticed, the man, now very old, walked on slowly unhurriedly, smiling beneath the sky, beneath the stars, happily carrying out his task…

FIVE

"'Ere you mister. You a tramp?" shouted a little gang of boys as they hurtled past the old man sitting on a bench. They didn't throw stones this time. It wasn't that they were afraid to, they just didn't want to - because this tramp was different. For a start, they hadn't seen him before, he didn't smell and he had a strange smile, fixed naturally on his face, which looked invulnerably peaceful.

Some of the children turned back – even though they'd be missing a good game, probably. They didn't really know why. They had jeered and scoffed, laughed and taunted at literally hundreds of people, not just tramps – though tramps were the easiest – but the children had not really been smiled at or smiled like that themselves, in a very long time. When the children reached the park bench where the old man was sitting, they smiled nervously.

The old man told the children that he had thought about it and yes, he probably was a 'tramp' because he had *tramped* all over the country for more years than he cared to remember. And anyway 'tramp' was as good a name as any.

The children laughed out loud. The tramp was funny. Fancy wanting to be called 'tramp,' they thought. But the man's smile never wavered, not for a moment. The children

L. Peter Jones

instinctively knew that this man was not afraid. Not afraid of anything – them or anything however old he was, and all the old men were *old*. It was remarkable – like his smile was remarkable.

The children decided they liked their new tramp. So they stayed with him sitting on the park bench.

Then the old man asked them if they would like to hear some stories. Some of the older children groaned aloud but inside they were as eager as the rest, they just did not want to show it, that's all.

"My stories could certainly teach you a thing or two," said the old man, still smiling serenely.

As soon as the old man had finished speaking, some very strange things started to happen to the children. First came the goose pimples. Then, a funny feeling in the pit of the stomach, which eventually made their heads tingle. And finally, they felt their hair stand on end.

Magic.

"'Once upon a time…'" began the old man, now surrounded by seated children, who, only moments before, had had nothing better to do than insult an old man.

"Is this true, Mister?" asked the tiny little voice from the front before the old man could continue. He must have been six years old, his nose was running, his knees were scuffed and his elbows were all scratches and sores. "'Cos me Mum don't like me listenin' to no lies…"

All the children laughed together. The old man smiled. The young boy who had interrupted the old man's story knew that smile. He remembered it suddenly. It was the smile of his Mother before she started shouting at him, when he was about two.

Cracks, Doors, Windows and a Story-Telling Tree

The boy started to cry. The old man held out his hands and the boy came over and sat next to him. No one thought it weird. Nor were they jealous. They knew that what was happening was right. They knew, everyone of them, in some strange way, that they, too, were crying like that boy and that they, too, had got up and sat next to the old man, and they, too, had been consoled and helped by him.

Real magic.

When the old man spoke again, they noticed his voice as if for the first time. It was like waking up to the Summer holidays.

It was a magical voice.

It was a deep voice, sonorous, warm and kind. A voice like a voice belonging to someone you have always loved. It was a voice, which rumbled and boomed in a quiet, pleasant kind of way. It was a voice, which had all the time in the world. A voice, which savoured every word and wasted none. A voice, which knew life, a voice which celebrated being alive. A Real Friend's voice!

But it was also a commanding voice, a voice of authority, a voice, which knew exactly what it was talking about. And the sound of that voice rolled on through every child's body so that every cell, every fibre and every nerve vibrated to every single word, which was being said.

This was magic – the everyday magic of the real.

The children were all amazed. They listened, fascinated.

The old man started with the story of the ant. Somehow it was the first thing he thought of. The old man then asked the children what story they would like to hear next. They all took it in turns so that it was fair. And everyone had his story told for him. They all knew that they had been heard, they all felt special.

And then, suddenly, it was time to go home. Where had the time gone?

"Will you be here tomorrow?" they all asked, and the old man, his eyes sparkling, slowly nodded. He was smiling exactly as he had when they had first seen him. And then they all disappeared, running home for tea or tears, the T.V., videos or being beaten because they should never have talked to strangers.

The next day most of the children returned, some had even brought brothers and sisters, one had brought his Mum, who was all tight-lips and folded arms until she heard the old man talk. She stood and listened, almost but not quite jealous of the children sitting next to the old man. Then she sat down as close as she dared to the old man and listened, quiet tears flooding her eyes.

Real Magic.

To begin with, the old man told them the story of the snail, which they found as fascinating as all the other stories he had told them the day before. They promised the old man that they would never catch snails and smash them for fun from now on. The old man smiled even more deeply, if that were possible.

The next day still more children came and more adults, too, though it was the adults who were most wary, the adults who were most afraid.

They soon forgot their fear, however, when they saw the old man, his smile, his love. They listened, enthralled, to his voice hearing the story uniquely as if it were told only to them.

Cracks, Doors, Windows and a Story-Telling Tree

Some brought a picnic and wandered off after a while to think about the story the had just heard but they always came back, perhaps more thoughtful, perhaps a little lighter, happier. Certainly people left the old man understanding a little more about this strange place of a planet we call home.

In this way the whole Summer passed. The children's Summer holidays. Everyone had heard hundreds of stories and still there could have been more. They listened and learned and listened and unlearned and listened and relearned. And finally they began to understand that everything really is just one great big story.

The old man knew that it was time to move on again, because school had started and he knew he would not be seeing the children again. It was turning cold, too. And for the first time since he had begun his task he felt ill-at-ease. Something at the not-too-far-back of his mind was trying to tell him something.

It had been a delight telling some of the stories he had heard himself, somewhere, somehow, a long, long time ago. But it really was time to move on.

Before he left, however, a car stopped and some smart men in uniforms got out and told him to get in. They were very efficient, and very tall. The car was amazing. It was fast and sleek and everyone inside the car was very proud of it. He could tell that, even if he were only a 'tramp'. He kept smiling all the way to the police station.

After the policeman had asked him some questions, they took him to a room which was very white and sparse, but lovely and warm. He spent a very pleasant night's sleep there. There was food and water and even a very hygienic toilet. In the morning he showered and they gave him some clean clothes. They were very kind. And he thanked them for all their kindnesses.

Before he left he was told to "move on" and he promised he would. And that was the truth for it is what he had been doing now for many, many years – so long he had forgotten how long. As he left there was one who lingered a little longer than the others. The old man stopped deliberately to let the young one, in his smart uniform, come to him. The young one tried to give him some money. But he refused with a small laugh. "All is provided for," he said, smiling at the young man's extravagance and seeing into his innocent heart. Some words from a long forgotten song came into his mind "All you need is love!" he said.

And the old man really did move on, even though he said smiling to himself that he was too old for this business now.

And by and by, the old man came to parts he knew from many long years ago. And he stopped. He looked around. There used to be a house, he knew, in that derelict plot. He smiled.

The old man also knew that at the bottom of the garden grew the most magical of trees. Now he had seen many trees and many strange things on his journeys but he had always remembered this tree as a good and faithful friend. The old man continued in the slow, unhurried way he had.

"Hmpf," said the tree in a booming kind of way that an old tree would have, "You've come back at last!"

"I suppose I have," said the old man.

"I can see you've forgotten your name," the tree commented.

"Yes it took rather a long time, but I managed it in the end!"

Cracks, Doors, Windows and a Story-Telling Tree

"So you know who you are at last?"

"Yes!" said the man, smiling a huge smile that radiated all the way to the stars…and back.

"Come! Tell me your story," said the tree, smiling.

So the old man sat down beneath that immense old tree and told his story. It took a long time to tell and a long time to listen. But the old man managed, even though, at the end, the old man had almost no voice left and certainly no more time. But before his task was complete, the man asked the tree for a final favour.

"What is it you want, little brother?" asked the tree, knowing full well what the favour was and that it would also be granted.

"Can I dig a hole here?" asked the man, smiling. "A hole that is as deep as your roots? I would like to be with you for all time."

"My roots are very deep," answered the tree, still smiling. "You must do what you feel is right; do what you will. But remember this, little brother, you will be with me forever, wherever you now rest your head."

The old man nodded, knowing, smiling.

The old man took his time to dig the hole and when it was done, he lay down in it.

And while stars traced their paths across the sky, the tree's leaves fell, and filled the hole completely.

END

Lightning Source UK Ltd.
Milton Keynes UK
UKHW031948090919
349468UK00001B/6/P